I0546985

BE NOT
DECEIVED

MICHAEL P. EARNEY

This is a work of fiction. Names, characters, places and incidents either are the product of the author's imagination or are used fictitiously, and any resemblance to actual persons, living or dead, business establishments, events, or locales is entirely coincidental.

Book design by Michael Earney and Lynn Amos
Cover design by Michael Earney & Kathleen's Graphics

All rights reserved. This book, or parts thereof, may not be reproduced without permission, except in the case of brief quotations embodied in critical articles and review.
Quote from Gary P. Nunn's *London Homesick Blues*" used by permission.

Copyright © 2017, 2020 Michael P. Earney

ISBN-13: 978-1941345573
ASIN: B01LDVARRK

Canyon Lake, Texas
www.ErinGoBraghPublishing.com

This book is licensed for your personal enjoyment only: it may not be re-sold or given away to other people. If you would like to share this book with another person, please purchase an additional copy for each recipient. If you are reading this book and did not purchase it, or it was not purchased for your use only, then please return to your favorite book retailer and purchase your own copy.

Thank you for respecting an author's work.

BONUS!
The short story, **R.I.P.** is included here, just as it was
with the first Matt Grey story, **Corpus**--just in case you
didn't buy **Corpus**

About the Author

Connect

Other Titles by Michael Earney

Chapter 1

Jasmine's dilemma

"Just how much longer do you think you can go on like this, Jazz?" Tony had been calling regularly, getting on her case. "You're on your feet, what, 12, 14 hours a day? You said yourself your varicose veins are killing you," he continued. "That rust-bucket you're driving's held together with baling wire." An exaggeration, but keeping the old thing running did cost more than it was worth. "You've no insurance. What if either one of you was to get sick? When was the last time you had a checkup? Checkup, what's that? What about Natalie, when was the last time she saw a doctor? When she was born?" He painted the bleakest of pictures, frustrated by Jasmine's seeming lack of concern. Of course, she worried about such things, but she valued her hard-won freedom and independence. She had reason to be proud of how she had managed to build the life that they had. But it was true, she was nearing forty. Some kind of change was inevitable. She owed Tony a lot.

While she accepted his help only under the direst of straits, and he never knew the half of them, his generosity to 'his little Natalie' had meant that she always had the books she needed, never missed out on school trips and could participate in all the normal activities of school life.

"I know you never complain. Natalie never complains. You ought to complain! There's no need for life to be so hard."

But the delicate balance of their existence would likely collapse completely if any change were imposed. That was Jasmine's dilemma. Get a proper job? 'Beware of any enterprise that requires new clothes.' I believe it was Will Rogers said that. New clothes, new car, new schedule, new expenses: she couldn't even afford to get into the position to apply for a position, and what would she do? she had little work experience outside of waitressing, knew next to zero about computers, nor did she want to know. All she wanted was a quiet life in her own little world— the one that she had painstakingly created.

***

Jasmine Allan was born and raised in a small fishing town just east of the Sabine River that separates Louisiana from Texas. Her father was a shrimper. He had come to the United States from Sicily as a young boy with his parents. From old photographs it would appear that her grandparents had been quite well off. Not the lowly Italian immigrants fleeing poverty for the New World like so many of their fellow countrymen portrayed in the history of those times. It was rumored, whether the invention of envious neighbors or simply family lore, that they were Mafioso.

Why they came to Louisiana was a mystery. Whatever they might have had they lost in the Depression. Her parents never spoke about it. Jasmine could only conjecture from little hints, evasions and abrupt silences that followed any questions she asked on the subject. Whatever connections her grandfather might have had seemed not to have carried over to his son. Jasmine's parents were hard-working, simple folk and Jasmine grew up poor, but ate shrimp every way it could be prepared and never stopped liking it. You don't know you're poor when everyone around you lives the same way as you. Jasmine's brother Tony, being the first born and a boy, received a stricter upbringing than "daddy's little princess". She was doted upon and allowed to do whatever she pleased. Some times to her mother's dismay. Of local, pioneer stock, her mother did not have such a permissive view of parenthood. Growing up, Tony took care to keep his sister out of trouble as much as he could, partly in order to keep himself out of trouble with his father. The need to be responsible was imposed upon him early; being dutiful and serious became second nature. Their age difference, their different dispositions and the fact that Tony moved away even before Jasmine, meant that they barely knew one another, other than as children. However, Tony never lost his concern and sense of responsibility for his sister. He admired her for choosing the lifestyle she had, for her independence and rejection of everything he thought of as "normal." They always kept in touch if only at long distance.

Jasmine became a teenager in the 60's. The world changed for most teens at that time and the rock'n roll revolution made it to the little village Jasmine called home. She and her best friend Becky started skipping school, smoking marijuana, drinking, and staying out late partying. Everything seemed possible. At sixteen they ran away from home, heading straight for the nearest big city, Houston. Things could have gone terribly wrong. But the solid, honest, family values they'd grown up with stuck with them. It was the age of Aquarius and they experimented with LSD, marijuana, alcohol and cocaine. They tried them all but, developed no addictions or dependencies. Heroin, luckily, was not as readily available or as popular as it is these days.

They worked hard, at the ever-available fallback job many girls and boys find themselves in at some point in their lives, waiting table. Though usually one most want to get out of as soon as possible. Jasmine and Becky actually enjoyed it and got good at serving; in later years Jasmine would proudly display her ability to carry six plates at a time without spilling a drop. They were both good-looking girls so tips were usually generous. Jasmine was on her way to becoming a beautiful woman. They rarely had to buy their own drinks when they went out and both had enough sense not to get into trouble. They were both virgins and, in spite of all the come-ons, passes, innuendos and dirty jokes that seemed to be an unavoidable part of the job, were still quite naïve and impressionable. So, when the handsome, popular, swaggering 22-year-old lead guitarist of their favorite band picked out Jasmine from the field of admiring fans, it was hard for her to resist. He swept her up into the band's entourage, installed her in the exalted place of "his lady" and took her virginity. After a few months of wild sex (which she found she enjoyed a lot) and late-night partying (not so much), Jasmine's innate conservatism and sense of rightness re-established itself and she moved on.

She and Becky went to Austin where the music was better, the city a more congenial place to be, and an altogether different sensibility prevailed. Austin was still a small city then, a university town where student taste set the tone. Many never graduated but became perennial students. Along with the constant influx of new students. For blocks in all directions, student housing, faculty housing, fraternity and sorority houses, hangers-on and wannabes surrounded the University. Guadalupe Street, "The Drag", as it was known, traversed the west side of the campus, ground zero for every kind of coffeehouse, pub, head-shop, café, restaurant and street vendor, virtually all featuring live music. Those who didn't play inside played on the street.

The girls found an apartment on Pearl Avenue, just blocks from Guadalupe and the park along Shoal Creek. They had very little reason to spend money on entertainment: there were always plenty of parties; free recitals, talks and gallery openings, and events at the university expanded their intellects. Richie, Jasmine's ex-boyfriend, often came up to Austin to play and as they had remained friends and sometime lovers, he was the girls' passport to just about all the clubs and performances in town where they met local musicians and promoters. There was still an easy camaraderie born of the hippie, peace and love sensibility that had taken over much of the nation's youth and the world's, for that matter. Musicians from England and Europe found their way to Austin. Everyone wanted to be "home with the Armadillo," in the iconic words of Gary P. Nunn's hymn to the Lone Star State, with "the friendliest people and the prettiest women you've ever seen."

Jasmine was a good judge of character, but not too discriminating. When she married for love at 20, she soon found that she had fallen for a hard-working, but equally hard-living, free-spending, not too bright young man from West Texas who didn't fit in with the educated, artsy crowd Jasmine had become part of. This difference was what had attracted her to him. Her own lack of education or training of any kind often made her feel inadequate even though her quick intelligence allowed her to mingle at parties and add her two cents worth to the drunken, usually inane talk that passed for conversation.

By contrast, Chuck lacked the experience and quick-wittedness required to keep up with even first-year UT students. The challenge was to appear knowledgeable in the highly competitive atmosphere of privileged, oneupmanship, intellectual mind-fucking and sexual predation which prevailed in the university environment. Jasmine's beauty counted for a lot and her popularity allowed them as a couple to continue being part of the scene, for a while at least.

Chuck's boorishness, which turned aggressive when he was drinking, led to her being invited to girls only events and then to receiving invites overtly excluding him until they were shunned and actually on occasion, asked to leave otherwise open parties. Although she never blamed Chuck and defended him when her close friends said anything, they both knew what was happening. Jasmine went out less and Chuck, whose attitude was "good riddance to that lot of fucking fairies," went drinking with his work buddies. Jasmine was not about to give up all her friends and when Sarah and Jennifer, members of Alpha Delta Pi sorority asked her to their annual AIDS benefit, she accepted as she had on previous occasions.

Predictably, Chuck refused to have anything to do with "those queers and dykes" and said he wasn't about to have her going either. Jasmine, who wasn't about to be dictated to and didn't share his views, went anyway. When she got home afterwards, a thoroughly drunk Chuck, in an attempt to apply the lowest denominator of male authority, resorted to self-righteous violence. Jasmine had never been hit by anyone before and determined she never would be again. She moved out the next day and returned to being room-mates with Becky. Jasmine was totally unswayed by Chuck's pleas and apologies, had a court order placed on him, and initiated divorce proceedings. After less than a year of marriage she was single again.

Chapter 2

Wimberley, Texas—life in the Hill Country

The spell was broken, however, and Austin was losing its charm. Becky had gotten a job with Dell and was partying much less than before. Jasmine continued waitressing. Tips were good, she could choose her hours, the social interaction kept her interest and she was good at it. Fran, a girl she met through work, was a surfer. The Gulf coast of Texas is not exactly known for surf, but there are plenty of opportunities to catch some decent waves and plenty who will make that three-hour drive for the chancc. Fran wcnt down to the coast as often as she could, Jasmine went along on occasion, learned to surf, and enjoyed being at the beach; having grown up by the water she missed it terribly, living in the city wasn't something she'd ever fully embraced. But she really couldn't afford to get into the whole scene, surfboards cost too much as did driving to the coast on the weekend when the restaurant was at its busiest and the owners often took advantage of Jasmine's reluctance to say no.

Still, they hung out a lot. Fran had a little cabin in the Hill Country outside of Austin and when she decided to go to Oahu and surf for a while she asked Jasmine if she would like to house-sit her place. Jasmine had spent a few pleasant weekends at the cabin, where it was clear to Fran that her friend was taken with the place. the very laid back, slacker atmosphere was even more pronounced out there than in Austin, which suited Jasmine just fine.

Wimberley is a small town, an hour from Austin and something of a tourist attraction. It's located at the confluence of the Blanco River and Cypress Creek which is fed by Jacob's Well, a clear, cold, artesian spring coming from deep within the limestone substrata. The spring, just outside of town, provides the much-needed influx of water to the Blanco which, by the summer time and often long before, earns its name when so much of the riverbed becomes exposed, dry white limestone. Places to get into the water and cool off are at a premium during the Texas summer. The tall, green Cypress trees along the water add much needed shade. Add to the mix quaint houses, antique stores, restaurants, live music and galleries and you have a place that draws a lot of people. It wasn't hard for Jasmine to find a job. Naturally, work was heaviest on the weekends and somewhat seasonal, so pay was less but the tips were good. With a smaller overhead Jasmine made ends meet and actually started to save a little.

The fact that she was pregnant was a matter of some concern, although Jasmine took it all in stride and never mentioned it to Chuck on the one occasion that he called drunk, from Sweetwater in West Texas to where he had returned. How he obtained her number she never knew; one of their mutual friends let it slip out or had been browbeaten into divulging it. Chuck was good at wheedling things out of people. She took the opportunity to let him know, in no uncertain terms, that she wanted nothing more to do with him. She seldom saw or spoke to the friends they had in common in Austin and decided that when the time was right she would tell the child about his or her father and where he most likely could be found. Becky was fully supportive of her decision but, took it upon herself to tell Tony. It was Becky, in fact, who had kept Tony aware of Jasmine's situation and circumstances through the years.

For some weeks before and after her daughter Natalie was born, Jasmine was unable to work. The money Tony sent got them through a period that, while happy, (Jasmine was delighted with her precious baby) was also one of stress and difficulty. Maria's restaurant, where Jasmine worked was owned by Mexican-Americans who had no problem accommodating another child into their already large family. Though proud and fiercely independent, Jasmine soon accepted that most of the day-to-day care of her child would be in the hands of the three Hinajosa girls and a grandmother or two.

Natalie grew up speaking almost as much Spanish as English, or at least the Texas Spanglish a lot of Tex-Mexicans speak. Jasmine never picked up much more than *hola, adios, buen provecho* and the names of the Mexican dishes served at the restaurant. Jasmine enjoyed working there and learned to cook many of the dishes served there. She helped cater parties and gallery openings which further integrated her into the local culture. Still, Jasmine was not that much of a joiner, she enjoyed her solitude outside of work. she lived by her senses. She read to learn rather than for entertainment though her learning came mostly from magazines, didn't watch much television other than movies of which she was a great fan, and the weather channel. She seldom watched the news—it upset her too much. She didn't want to know who was killing who or what politician had his hand in the till or down whose panties. She didn't want all the world's evils and corruption polluting her mind. She gleaned enough of what went on in the world from her customers. The movies she watched were non-violent, if not, she turned them off. A true child of the 60's she still asked, "Whatever happened to peace, love and understanding?" She was not an airhead, in many ways she was too tuned-in, too empathetic, sensitive to all around her and self-aware enough to know what made her happy and what did not. She chose to surround herself with those in tune with her viewpoint. Day to day life exposed her to enough ugliness without bringing it into her home.

Fran finally concluded she was never going to leave Oahu and offered to sell the Wimberley cabin to Jasmine. As usual, Jasmine managed to find a way and worked out a long-term payment arrangement they both were happy with. Now she had a home of her own; a place of peace, harmony and love; a shelter for herself and Natalie, an antidote to the outside world she couldn't control.

Her openhearted, trusting and generous nature brought out the best in people. When Natalie was almost a teenager, a long overdue addition to the cabin was needed—it had been barely adequate for one. Friends, many of them skilled plumbers, electricians and carpenters, pitched in for an old-fashioned barn-raising. Most of them were regulars at the restaurant where Jasmine's cheerful countenance and easy banter were often the highlight of their day. Kindness was met with kindness, favor for favor. She bartered, helped and was helped; garage-sales, bake-sales, wherever a bargain was to be had, Jasmine would find it.

She recycled what others threw away or thought worthless. She always dressed stylishly and colorfully in the finest cast-offs to be found and made sure Natalie was always well-dressed too. People knew she was poor and, while that's not a crime in the United States of America, it's frequently frowned upon. In the Texas Hill

Country large estates, Mac-mansions and second homes were the norm. There were many others who struggled to survive like Jasmine, and many in better circumstances that envied her. But she was content with her life.

Wimberley continued to grow, bringing more tourists and more development. The monthly flea market attracted so many visitors that getting through town on the weekend that it was held, was a real headache. More businesses opened or expanded and traffic increased. During the summer Jasmine worked as many hours at the restaurant as she could and mostly stayed home when she wasn't working: partly to avoid the crowds and partly to save money for the winter months when it was mostly locals that showed up at the restaurant and her income dropped off. Still, she was happy: Natalie was a good and dutiful daughter. Together they fit into the community. Her garden, made up of transplants, propagated cuttings, scavenged throwaways and pickings from the gardens of friends, thrived under her care. During the summer months conserving water was often mandated, and was a practice she followed anyway, in order to keep her water bill low. During winter freezes she moved as many plants as possible into the house.

Love-life was spasmodic. There wasn't a large pool of men to choose from and there were plenty of other ladies in town pretty much in the same position, who were more flexible and less discriminating. She steered clear of married men.

The town was far too small to avoid gossip and a single, good-looking, unwed mother had enough to contend with. She never had men stay over unless Natalie was at camp or sleep-over with a friend and even then, it had to be a very special circumstance.

When a relationship showed signs of being long-lasting she would let Natalie give the thumbs-up or -down, knowing she herself was more likely to see the good in someone, missing the flaws that her girl picked up on. Every so often a new man would move into town or a visitor would live sufficiently close that driving back and forth wasn't a problem. In the end the bond she and Natalie had meant more to her than any relationship. Even offers of marriage and security, which were made on more than one occasion, ultimately lacked the incentives her practical nature and Natalie's intuition needed to make such a dramatic change.

Chapter 3

Time of change

The winter of '98 was a hard one. Mother and daughter both had heavy bouts of the 'flu. Becky, knowing Jasmine wouldn't have money to spend on doctors, and, if she had, would spend it on Natalie rather than herself, and fearing that one or the other of them would develop pneumonia, once again called Uncle Tony. Still in Houston, his business flourishing, he was only too happy to help. This was how things had come to the point where Tony decided to take matters his own hands. His unceasing reiteration of all the things that he saw as wrong in her life, the state of her car, her health, her lack of savings, was his way of trying to help. "Can't go on, Jazz. Think of Natalie." That was the ace that Tony always pulled out. Think of Natalie! She had always thought of Natalie. She had always discussed with Natalie matters that governed their life. Natalie knew her mother loved her life the way it was and loved her mother for it. But Natalie was changing. Her needs were different. She was inclined to agree with her

Uncle Tony. Her sheltered life no longer had the appeal it had when she was growing up.

When Tony insisted on introducing her to his friend Jack, a wealthy retired realtor from Houston now living in the Hill Country, Jasmine had run out of excuses to resist.

Jack Fellini had been born and grew up in Houston. He had made a lot of money in real estate and instead of continuing to work to make more money, had retired early. Fellini (no relation, unfortunately—that might have made him a bit interesting), knew only that there had been a movie director by that name, had never seen one of his films: wasn't interested; wasn't interested in much of anything. The only surprising thing about him was his decision to buy a small, 900-acre ranch.

"Whatever possessed him?" Jasmine asked Tony.

"I don't know—must have watched too many episodes of 'Dallas'." said Tony who wouldn't dream of leaving Houston for a place in the middle of nowhere.

The ranch was on the Medina River, upstream from Castroville. In fact, the Texas Hill Country attracted many people who had spent their working lives in Houston or Dallas. It is second only to Florida as the most popular place to retire in the USA. Having no desire to move to Florida, Fellini had used his realty connections to zone in on the hot place in Texas to live.

Castroville had been settled in 1844 by families brought over from Alsace and Baden. Well into the 20th century Alsatian was as likely to be heard spoken as English. The building of Medina dam and the resulting creation of Medina Lake had made the area a popular recreational destination and the Medina Valley became more agriculturally productive than it had been when first settled. Castroville wasn't so very different from where she already lived. Yet it seemed a long way from anywhere, certainly far from any of her friends. The nearest big city, San Antonio, was only 26 miles from Castroville, but she knew almost no-one there, having little reason to visit when she lived less than 50 miles away. Austin had continued to be the city she went to whenever the desire to experience the bright lights came over her. The dullness of the man and the thought of being isolated with him out on the ranch threw her into a panic. He was prepared to pay for Natalie to go to college, so Jasmine wouldn't even have her company. She was getting plenty of support and encouragement, though not to do what she wanted to do. The man certainly seemed enamored of her; either that or he owed Tony big time.

Casting around desperately for a way out, or at least a delaying strategy, Jasmine recalled something an ex-boyfriend had once told her, "Never get too involved with someone until you've been on a trip with them." In that case, he may have been referring to a mushroom or acid trip, but either way, it applied. Jasmine had only been out of the country once, and technically that hadn't been out of the country since she had visited Fran in Oahu, where she had almost succumbed to the siren call of the surf, herself. So, she proposed a trip together, purely platonic, to Sicily. She knew that there were supposedly relatives there and she had always wanted to see where her parents and grandparents had come from. She had even fantasized that perhaps she could live there. Anyway, it was a way to attain a long-held dream and afford a perfect excuse to end the whole affair—unless by some miracle they proved to be compatible.

Fellini refused point-blank. Not Italy. He proposed Cabo San Lucas, the Virgin Islands, Thailand, Bali. Jasmine was tempted but, remained equally adamant—Sicily. Finally, reluctantly, he agreed. She wanted to keep her indebtedness to him as low as possible so that she could break it off with as good a conscience as possible, but he insisted on opening an account for her so that she could have her own credit card, something she had never had before. All arrangements and reservations were to be made in her name. They would rent a car or go with a chauffeur/guide only. There were certain towns that could not be included in their itinerary. While he was willing to indulge her desire to seek out relatives, he was not going to seek out any of his own, and he knew where they lived. His parents, much to his chagrin, had kept contact with a whole family tree of relatives in Sicily and the mainland that he said would occupy their entire time there if it were known he was visiting.

"You visit one aunt and not another and it's a snub. You never hear the end of it. Plus, you'll gain about 20lbs. If you don't eat everything they put in front of you it's another affront. It ain't, gonna, happen."

Jasmine was thrilled by the thought that unknown cousins, uncles and aunts might be as warm and welcoming to include her in family activities, and she set about narrowing down the places where they could be found.

"Okay, here's the deal." Jack had become increasingly agitated as the date of their departure had neared. Now, as they were headed for San Antonio airport, he spoke up. "Never refer to me as anything other than Jack. As far as anyone need know, we are Mr. & Mrs. Allan."

Jasmine had kept her married name, never having liked 'Vigliano' which nobody could ever pronounce properly, and when she was growing up kids had their fun with, 'Miss Piggy Ano' and 'Jasmine Biggybutto' being some of the more tasteful.

"You tell no-one where I'm from, what I do—not anything—make stuff up if you have to. Better you just say nothing."

"For heaven's sake, how am I going to do that?" Jasmine exclaimed.

"Improvise then," he snapped. "Say I'm Italian from Argentina, Italian-speaking Swiss— anything will do for casual conversation. Anyone starts getting too curious, let me know. I'll deal with it then. Work on it while we're on the plane. We've a lot of hours ahead of us before we arrive."

Boy, a great start to a trip she had looked forward to for so long without knowing that it could ever happen. But she was not going to let anything ruin her vacation. She hated to lie, but she could make up all kinds of stories. Keeping them straight was always the problem, but most people they wouldn't meet more than once. When she was alone there would be no problem. He had already told her she would have to go to some places on her own; a driver would take her. That suited her fine. She didn't want to be constrained or evasive with family members she was sure she would find. It just seemed so petty and dull of Fellini to be so against meeting new people, making new friends, having new experiences. If only she could have done this with Natalie. They would have had lots of fun!

Chapter 4

Sicily

Palermo airport was pandemonium. There were tearful good-byes, joyous greetings. Children ran and screamed, mothers screamed and corralled. Fathers barked imprecations that were largely ignored. If nothing else, Italians were loud!

The little hotel Jack had found for them was, by contrast, a haven of peace tucked away on a tiny square where a few old ladies sat and gossiped. Jack had seemed nervous as officials at the airport scrutinized their passports, but now was relaxed and smiling for what seemed like the first time since they'd left the ranch. His Italian was a little rusty, but the owner of the hotel, a plump, short lady of about Jasmine's age, had remarked on his Sicilian accent.

"You never told me you spoke Italian," Jasmine said as they sat out on the small balcony of their room, drinking a light local wine the owner had suggested.

"There's a lot you don't know about me," Jack said, and perhaps realizing that he wasn't exactly sounding friendly, continued, "I don't get to speak it much anymore. It's all we spoke when I was growing up. My grandma, my mom's mother, lived with us till she died, she never did learn English."

"That must have been nice," said Jasmine.

"Pays off sometimes," Jack replied with a shrug. Subject closed. Conversation ended. It seemed to Jasmine that he didn't really want to get to know her. All her attempts to draw him out were met with the same kind of response. Monosyllabic, as though it was too much effort. Jasmine was used to chatting. It might be mindless for the most part, but it helped people to know one another and be relaxed around each other. She believed it had helped her through the hours of waitressing and it had made her many friends.

Jasmine was up early the next morning, determined to get the most out of what she considered to be her once-in-a-lifetime opportunity to see Sicily and meet long-lost relatives. She knew the name of the village where her grand-parents were from and their family's names, but little more. The village was on the east coast, so they would make their way there as they visited the main places she had on her list.

As Jack was inclined to have a leisurely breakfast with the paper, Jasmine ventured out alone on their first morning and right away found an English-speaking taxi driver who agreed to take her up the Monte Pellegrino. There was a stunning view of the Bay of Palermo and the Lipari islands, and the ancient buildings they passed wiped out the sight of city squalor skirted on the way. The mountains, the blue of the Mediterranean, and the warm sea breezes coming all the way from North Africa were enough to blow away any misgivings she might still harbor. She felt at ease, like she fitted in here.

During the following days she would marvel at the architecture, the landscape, the food and the people. It was all quite over-whelming. Even Jack was impressed. He was constantly on the look-out for pickpockets, scippatore he called them, bag-snatchers,—they took wallets, watches, jewelry, anything they could grab. He complained about the lack of road signs and the way Sicilians drove, but it was clear he was going through a profound mental change.

Sicily was like nothing either of them had experienced or imagined. Despite centuries of invasion, and even with the ruins of the Romans, Greeks, and Saracens, the land was mostly untouched. Flowers covered the landscape and there were oranges and lemons everywhere. Almond trees were in blossom and olive groves seemed endless. Towns huddled on cliffs overlooking the sea, sat on precipitous mountain sides or crowded around exquisite beaches. From Palmina's ancient ruins and its views of snow covered Mount Aetna emitting its long plume of smoke, they went to the Cathedral in Cafalu, and from the cliffs there were more breathtaking views of the Lipari Islands. They visited the Madonna of Tears in Siracusa the port city of Catania, considered by many to be the most beautiful town in the world. The city's 2,700year history was reeled out for them by a friendly guide who insisted on showing them around. They went to the cathedral, which was once a Greek theater, had been converted into a mosque after the Muslim conquest, then restored by Norman invaders. They learned that Syracuse's most famous son, Archimedes, he of the "Eureka" moment, (he was taking a bath or something, was all Jasmine remembered about him), was killed by Roman invaders. Shortly after that titbit of historic information, Jasmine's eyes began to glaze over and the list of successive invasions went in one ear and out the other. She enjoyed the archeological museum, full of objects dug up on the island, from prehistoric times to the more recent past. More ruins, more churches, and always eating, eating. Seafood salads became Jasmine's favorite, closely followed by pasta con iricci, sea urchin, and the desserts! Zuccata, buccellato, cannoli, and the one Jasmine couldn't resist – cassata Siciliana.

Together with the array of ice creams and cheeses, she was afraid if her heart didn't give out first, she wouldn't fit into any of her clothes. The Arab occupiers had left their mark on the island in many ways, but one that Jasmine took to gratefully, was the wide, light cotton dresses.

Jasmine did get to visit the little village of her ancestors, where she was welcomed warmly. She spent one wonderful day with relatives who treated her like a queen. One cousin, Alfredo, had visited the States and spoke passable English. He translated as best he could, all the questions she had for them and all the offerings that the women, mostly great aunts, great nieces, pressed upon her. It was everything she had always imagined and more. but because of the language barrier and the cultural gap she had to accept she would never fit into their way of life. While addresses were exchanged and promises to stay in touch were made, it turned out to be the least satisfying part of her trip.

Jack had booked them into a villa nearby. It was an old farm, built in 1682 with grand solid stone walls, but completely modernized with a huge pool, luxurious bedrooms, sweeping views of the unspoiled Ragusan countryside and the Mediterranean. Jack elected to stay there and Jasmine couldn't help feeling dishonest descending from this luxury into her relatives' simple lives. But that was the only shadow on the stay—until that last day.

Chapter 5

Detective and would-be client finally meet

"This is Matt." If I had a secretary she would probably say, 'Matt Grey Detective Agency,' or 'Matt Grey & Associates, how may I direct your call?' I don't, I answer my own phone.

There was a moment's hesitancy, then a woman's voice said, "Mr. Grey, I very much need your help and I need you to bear with me on the, perhaps, unusual circumstances that I will explain as best I can, if you agree."

"I'll be happy to do the best *I* can if you'll explain a little more these "unusual circumstances". First of all, to whom am I speaking?"

"Well, that's the first of them," she replied with a slight laugh. "I got your number from a friend in Port Aransas who knows you. I'm calling from a public phone and for your own sake as much as mine I can't tell you my name or visit your office."

"This is not making it easy," I replied, though it was certainly intriguing.

"Could we perhaps meet in the restaurant at the museum this afternoon?"

I live in Corpus Christi, just down the road from Port Aransas, so the museum she was referring to was the Art Museum of South Texas at the end of the promenade on Shoreline Boulevard overlooking Corpus Christi Bay and the Ship Channel. We agreed upon a time and the caller hung up. Mystery woman, I thought—highly melodramatic, paranoid or batty. I've dealt with them all at different times.

At the appointed hour I took a table in the Dobson Café closest to the water. The restaurant was empty. After about five minutes a woman entered, dressed in a simple knee-length dress, carrying a large woven bag on her shoulder, a scarf and large dark glasses. I was about to rise, but the woman ignored me and went to sit two tables away.

***

After receiving her order, the waitress having gone inside, she said, "Mr. Grey, can you hear me well enough if I speak like this without facing you?" I turned my head to look out at the bay and said yes. "I'm going to leave a folder on the chair between us when I leave and it might be best if you read it before deciding whether you can, or want, to do anything else. I will tell you that everything in there is true and then you will appreciate the deadly seriousness of the matter. No-one else must see the contents and I must ask you to destroy them if you decide against taking the case. I do have the money to hire you if you decide to proceed. I will depend entirely on your discretion and decisions on how to solve this problem if, indeed, it can be solved." At that, she turned to me and said, "How do you like the work?" waving her hand towards the gallery space. We chatted briefly in the normal manner of two stranger's meeting in that kind of situation. My impression was of a sane but clearly stressed person, trying to maintain her composure.

The folder held an account, in great detail, of a couple's (no names were given) visit to Sicily; how, near the end of their vacation, the man had been stabbed in the stomach and his throat cut, in the street by a total stranger. The woman had witnessed the murder from an upstairs window, and would never forget the look the assailant had given her, although she had told the police she had not seen the man's face.

Before being interviewed by the police, she had called her brother in Houston, who told her to leave immediately, get her daughter who was in her first semester at University of Georgia in Athens, and to disappear completely. The woman hadn't known if she was allowed to leave the country, but the event and the urgency of her brother's insistence was enough.

The inspector in charge of the case had a car take her back to the hotel, where she packed her bags and made a reservation to fly out that night. There was no way she would spend another night in that room, even without the fear that she might also be the target of a deranged killer still at-large. The fact that their bookings had been made in her name made things easier, and having the money to pay the extra charge for the changes was a relief, but nothing could take away from the horror of her companion's murder.

She had tried to keep her mind from replaying the incident, but no matter how she tried to concentrate on the present moment the memory of watching helplessly as her friend fell to the ground would not go away. That she might be accosted by someone meaning her harm, stopped by the police, or even a random stranger wanting nothing more than directions or a handout, had kept her wound tight until she was finally seated in the plane for the return flight.

She began to relax; idly watching the other passengers' futile search for room in the overhead compartments and to ultimately jostle their overstuffed bags into the too small spaces.

Then she had seen him: nonchalantly making his way down the aisle, looking neither to left or right. It was the assassin, she was sure of it! The way an animal instinctively knows when a predator lurks, her body was sure, even if the dark glasses and casual vacation apparel made him look like any other of the homeward-bound Americans filling their seats. His impassive face had filled her with more dread than if he had snarled at her. She began to tremble as the shock of the sight of him, and all that it implied, hit her.

Still, she'd had enough presence of mind to show no reaction and look down, repressing the urge to peer between the seats to see where he went to sit. Slowly the reality of her situation had sunk in—a nightmare reality. Trapped in a capsule for what seemed like an eternity under normal conditions was now compounded. A nightmare where she would be afraid to sleep, go to the bathroom, read, or even eat without gagging.

For the first time, she hoped that the annoying security procedures at airports were effective, although she knew the man would not need a weapon if he was able to get close enough to her. How was it, she found herself wondering, that the incident of the terrorist attack in New York, horrendous though it was, had brought about this seemingly world-wide elaborate system. She'd heard that even bus stations in Mexico had the same procedures. Compared with much of the mayhem in the world, why had this single event precipitated such activity? Could the USA's Homeland Security department have such power as to require conformity around the globe? Had the airlines colluded in demanding them? Could each country have independently put in place these identical installations?

The woman realized how appallingly ignorant she was about things that had previously had no relevance to her life. She vaguely recalled hearing that there were marshals placed on airliners to protect travelers, but how would she know who that was among the hundreds of passengers aboard. She could hardly call one of the hostesses and say that the man in B64 was possibly planning to kill her.

As she sat running one elaborate scenario after another through her mind, it slowly dawned on her that the man sitting next to her had been trying to engage her in conversation. Just as she had invented stories for her partner, she could invent one about that man back there. And so, the woman told her seat neighbor that her ex-boyfriend, whom she had dumped after he had forced her to perform an act she dared not describe, was now stalking her and was on the plane. Together they formulated a plan in which, when they arrived in Houston, she would push her way to the door while her collaborator would block any advance from those behind.

He assured her he would make certain that her "little boyfriend" would not get near her. His size, and the fact that he had played defensive tight-end at college, gave her enough relief that had actually allowed her to get a little sleep—after he had entertained her with tales of his football days. He had kept to himself some of the high-jinx he and his team-mates had gotten up to, especially those that involved cheerleaders doing things that might easily be similar to, if not the same as, that which the woman had hinted her supposed boyfriend had indulged himself in. He thought it best not to ask for her phone number, guessing that if they were to develop a relationship, he might find himself in the same position at some time in the future, recalling what, in retrospect, had been some pretty reprehensible behavior on his part towards young women in his past.

Just as planned, as soon as the seat belt sign had gone off, her burly savior stood blocking the aisle while she slipped out, grabbed her bags, gave him a peck on the cheek and, apologizing profusely, elbowed her way to the front. Once the door was open she had run up the passage and rushed to the customs and immigration. There, again thanks to Jack, who had insisted on buying them each the Global Entry pass, she was able to avoid the interminable line through customs, where her pursuer would have had no problem keeping her in sight. She phoned her brother while she sped through the crowds and poured out all that had happened. They both knew that her pursuer would only wait so long at the gate for the San Antonio connection, or he might have already anticipated that she wouldn't risk finding herself in the same plane with him again, now that she was obviously aware of who he was, and would be considering his own alternatives. The woman's brother had told her to take a cab over to Love Field and find a motel close to the airport, where her daughter would be arriving that night.

When she had called him from Palermo, he had booked a flight for her daughter, and so gave his sister the flight number and time. Her brother also said it was too big of a risk for them to go to his place there in Houston —stressing that they should probably leave town that same night if possible.

The woman expressed concern about her brother's safety, but he'd insisted he would be all right, assuring her there was no reason they would bother him.

She'd told her brother that the whole thing was totally inexplicable, she was a nervous wreck, and that her mind just kept running one nightmare scenario after another. He told her not to worry about him, to just do what he'd said and they'd be out of sight and out of mind in no time.

She had done just as her brother suggested and, since she was too distraught to sleep, after picking up her daughter at Love Field, drove to Victoria where they spent what was left of the night.

After reading the account I concluded that my would be client was the woman protagonist and that she had written in such detail in order to process the event and try to find some explanation, Either that or, so that I, reading it, would not think she was delusional.

***

It turned out that the credit card account that the man had opened for the woman was for a large amount of money, and that regular monthly deposits were being made into it. Presumably it was the source of my would-be client's income.

I've heard of blood feuds, vendettas, in Sicily going back generations. It could be something like that was happening here. But would there really be any reason for the woman to fear? Surely, pursuing a possible witness all the way across the Atlantic was unlikely, although the woman seemed convinced the man on the plane was her companion's killer. Apparently her brother accepted the possibility. Something else must be going on which would require a little homework.

As soon as you start looking into the history of Sicily, the Mafia begins to raise its ugly head. And the more I read, the uglier it got. Turns out the Mafia has been around for centuries, presumably growing out of family solidarity, tribalism, clans, secret societies that think of themselves as elite. The select, whose members have unique rights. They were never Mafia, only "friends", "men of honor" taking care of each other. You scratch my back, I'll scratch yours. Successive governments denied the existence of such an organization. After all, they were "friends" or friends of friends, owing their positions to the manipulative power of local bosses over the electoral process, the awarding of government grants and contracts, the selection of officials and the distribution of wealth.

It's said that the ease with which American forces entered Sicily at the end of the Second World War was facilitated through a deal with Lucky Luciano, a Mafia boss, from his jail cell in the U.S. Whether true or not, in 1943, the American military formally handed over legal power to those of the established hierarchy who were predominantly Mafia. Upon his release and return to Sicily, Lucky Luciano was made an honorary Colonel in the U.S. Army.

From that, the Mafia grew, boldly asserting its power, blatantly displaying their wealth, defying the laws, openly killing those that opposed them in order to cow any that might try. When Sicily's Mafia got into the drug trade it became a truly international organization. Europe's largest heroin refinery was in the Sicilian province of Trapani. In 1982, the city of Trapani shipped a third of a billion dollars' worth of heroin to Montreal via Paris. When it was shut down by crusading lawmen, the murder of judges, magistrates, investigators and critics became endemic.

With such high stakes, inter-mafia wars broke out. Toto Riini, who owned Trapani's refinery in a joint venture with Bernardo Brusca, was highly ambitious and apparently saw where the business was going. When he was nineteen, Riini had killed a friend and went on to kill some

800 more in a drive to become the absolute ruler of Sicily's Mafia. By the end of the 1980's he had achieved his goal. Just as with absolute despots throughout history, once the killing started there was no stopping! Like the Mugal ruler killing all the other princes in the harem once he was crowned, or Stalin eliminating any and all rivals. You can never be too careful. Paranoia takes over, anybody and everybody could be looking to replace you by the same method.

Did any of this have anything at all to do with what I had in front of me?

The most poignant part of the story was that on that last day the man had told the woman that he was glad they had come and thanked her for the great time he'd had. He told her that he was always scared growing up, had heard so many stories, and wanted her to know he was not afraid anymore. They were the last words he said to her before going out for the paper. She had gone to the window to call down and ask him to bring her a Pellegrino, only to witness his gruesome murder.

I wondered about the credit card account he had opened for her. Why was more money still coming into it and from where? Had he, from some fear, premonition or knowledge, planned to use the account after their return in order to disappear himself? There was obviously something that had made him resistant to going to Sicily in the first place, something that had plagued him while they were there. For good reason, as it turned out. And what about the brother: where did he fit in, and where was he? I needed some names.

While I waited for her to call again—I guess she was giving me time to think it over—I devoured everything I could find on Cosa Nostra, their incredible stranglehold on Italian society and the amazingly brave few who toiled for years in the face of corrupt judges, politicians, law enforcement, and a generally complacent or acquiescent public. I learned about the courageous prosecutors who persisted, and when they got too close were posted to Sicily on what they knew was an assignment to death, but still persevered until they were blown up, gunned down, "rubbed out" in some grizzly fashion or other. Their example inspired others who stepped in to continue the fight and slowly the wall of silence crumbled. In spite of the risks, some journalists and an emboldened public demanded an accounting.

Against all odds, Life Senator Guilio Andretti, 20-times Minister and seven-times Prime Minister of Italy, was finally tried for murder and his Mafia connections. Throughout, he adamantly denied ever having met Mafioso, even those with whom he had been photographed! He contradicted the evidence of eye-witnesses and the confessions of others involved. To admit to even one of the accusations would be to acknowledge a lifetime of indebtedness to the Mafia. Admission that his entire public life had been steeped in fraud and deception.

One over-riding inspiration of these "men of honor" was, ironically, to tell the truth, which explains why, perhaps, when a "penitent" Mafioso turned State's Evidence, he was completely frank about the mob's methods. One particularly gruesome detail that struck me was how Giovanni Brusca, son of the Trapani heroin refiner, also on trial in absentia, kidnapped the son of a *pentito*, had him strangled and then dissolved in acid — apparently a popular way of disposing of bodies. Any witness against the Mafia was under sentence of death for the rest of their life.

Perhaps the man in my client's life had somehow been in that position and her brother too. I had to consider all the possible scenarios I could think of.

I also asked my girlfriend, Kate, who had recently been promoted to deputy head of the forensics department in the Corpus Christi police department—we joked that one of these days she would make enough money to support the two of us—to watch out for any reports from Houston of homicides or suspicious-looking deaths of Italian males in the 50- to 60-year-old bracket during the last month and for the next few months (just in case).

"Is this the kind of thing you're looking for?" asked Kate, dropping a sheaf of paper on the dining room table.

"Wow, that was quick," I said.

"I want this case over with before anyone links you to the mystery lady," Kate replied.

I had told Kate everything I knew. Ever since we first met she has been my unpaid assistant, head cook and bottle washer in our little home business. She did not like this particular case one bit. I had stopped quoting from the material I was reading, but the damage was done.

"What do we have here," I said, leafing through the reports she had obtained from Houston. "Pizza parlor owner injured during attempted robbery; thieves escape with five pizzas. Carwash owner, Leonardo Alfieri, run over by car exiting wash before the wash cycle was complete; driver said he didn't realize he had his foot on the accelerator. Hit and run, Italian-surnamed victim. Hit and run, Italian-surnamed driver. Man asphyxiated trying to free himself from bonds; the victim was apparently tied up by robbers who broke into his apartment. Antony Vigliano, travel agent and longtime Houston resident, was found dead in his apartment which had been ransacked. He was bound hands and feet and appeared to have died trying to free himself."

"Can you get me a picture of the body at the crime scene on this one, sweetheart?" Something about this one set-off a little alarm bell. I try to listen to my instincts and usually regret it whenever I don't.

The next day my client called to set up a meeting for the following day. That evening Kate handed me a photo that had been faxed from Houston. It wasn't the best of prints, but it showed a man, his face bloated and distorted, who could have been between 50 and 60, lying on his side, his legs bent up behind him as were his hands, which were tied to his ankles—truly incapacitating and painful in the extreme. Also, a position virtually impossible to free oneself from, I would imagine. But could it kill you?

I gazed at the picture and let my eyes just take in the details. Then I saw what appeared to be a thin cord stretching from the man's feet to around his neck. This rang more bells and I went back to my growing stack of books. An hour later I found it: "*Incaprettamento*, a rural mafia method where a victim's hands and feet are bound behind the back, an attached rope is noosed around the neck, and as the muscles slowly yield, slow strangulation is the result (from *capretto*; a young kid goat, that was tied this way to take to market); also convenient for the trunk of a car. One of many ways to revenge, punish or warn."

Chapter 6

At the beach in Port Aransas, Texas

Our next meeting was on the second level of La Palmera Mall. I parked next to the tan '98 Taurus wagon as directed; after a few minutes the driver's door opened, the woman slipped out and climbed into the passenger seat of my old Buick. It was 3:30 in the afternoon. Without the large sunglasses she had worn during our meeting at the museum, I could see that the woman was beautiful, looked young for her age and had managed to keep in shape; her eyes showed a mixture of innocence, bewilderment and fear. I suspected she was suffering from post-traumatic stress disorder. Obviously, she had not been able to obtain any counseling and I now knew she had good reason to fear.

"Alright," I said, "I'm in. I think I know the dangers that might be involved—and I want to stress the 'might' as I'm not prepared, for the moment, to accept that you are in danger." I said this to try to allay her fears so that she might gain some relief, however fleeting it might be. "I have to have names. I assume Antony Vigliano is your brother."

She gasped and said, "Tony. Have you seen him, has anything happened?"

I wasn't about to tell her the truth and add to her distress. "No, but I need to know all you can tell me about him and about the gentleman you went to Sicily with, where you went, who you met there."

She slumped into her seat, relaxing perhaps for the first time since Sicily. "I'm sorry to say there is little I can tell you about Jack." She then told me the circumstances that led up to the trip. "I probably should have learned more," she sighed. "But my brother vouched for him. He wasn't that forthcoming and I wasn't that interested in him anyway. He did open up some in Sicily. I know his parents came from Ragusa—that much he told me."

"Okay, he sold real estate. Did he mention anyone he dealt with, developers, contractors, corporations?"

"Not that I can think of," she said.

"Well, try to remember anything you can." I didn't want to put pressure on her. "Tell me about Tony."

"I know it may sound strange, but I don't know a lot about his life either. He has a travel agency and travels a lot. He's always dating air hostesses," she added with a laugh. "He's always telling me that he could get me free flights to anywhere I wanted to go. I never had the money to travel. I did go to Hawaii once, but I had a free place to stay once I was there. I liked that," she said nostalgically. "He always wants to send me to resorts where everything is included, or on cruises, but those kinds of vacations never interested me."

This wasn't getting us anywhere. "Is your daughter with you?" A thought had occurred to me.

"Yes, Natalie's at home. I told her not to leave the house—I'm almost afraid to let her out of my sight," she replied. Natalie, it seemed, had spent more time talking to her uncle than her mother had. "I haven't told her about what happened on my trip," she blurted.

"What have you told her?"

"I said that Jack had reacted badly when I said I wouldn't marry him and that he naturally wouldn't continue paying her tuition. I had to think of something! Actually, Jack turned out to be a nice man, shy—I felt like he'd been hurt at some time but I never could fathom what it was that made him so apprehensive. Now I feel responsible for his death. If only I hadn't insisted on going to Sicily none of this would have happened." She began to cry, I encouraged her to let it out then remained silent until she regained her composure, at which she apologized. I told her there was nothing to apologize for and said she was better off letting it out than keeping it bottled up inside.

"Look, why don't I come over to the island tomorrow," (the island, meaning Port Aransas which is on Mustang Island, was locally understood), "meet Natalie, and if she's agreeable we can go down to the beach. It'll get her out of the house and give you some time to yourself. I'll explain what I can to her without getting into detail or upsetting her." Jasmine thought about it for a while with a skeptical expression. Then I could see that she realized what an enormous relief it would be and she agreed, though hesitantly.

Natalie looked a lot like her mother. Pretty, tall and gangly, still growing into her adult body, she was ready to go when I got to the house, with her beach bag, towel and lotion. It was a mark of Jasmine's trust in me that she let me make off with her teenage daughter and Natalie showed remarkable self-possession. There had probably been enough men come and go in Jasmine's life for Natalie to trust her mother's judgment.

She was silent during the short drive to the beach. I parked by the pier and she headed straight for the water. There were decent waves breaking so I grabbed the boogie board that Kate always kept in the car and headed down myself. I left the board with the towels and stuff and went in. I prefer to body-surf but, thought Natalie might like to use it. I yelled to her as such and she did go and get it. We spent a good hour, catching waves.

Back on the beach I waited for her to break the ice. "Mom says you're a detective. Is that true?"

"Yes, I am" I replied, "and I wanted to ask you something about your Uncle Tony."

"Oh, no! He's not dead, is he?" was her surprise response.

"Why do you ask that, Natalie?" I asked, somewhat taken aback.

"Well, something weird is obviously going on. I've never known mother to be in such a state. She won't tell me what it is, but it obviously has to do with Jack, which means Uncle Tony is involved."

"But why would you think he might be dead?" I asked.

"I don't know, it's like, I just feel that something terrible happened. Mom has never kept things from me, like I said, so it has to be big. Will you tell me what's going on?" I had the feeling that the girl was much more mature and capable of handling the truth than her mother gave her credit for. I decided to jump in feet first.

"Yes, your Uncle's dead," I said bluntly, "and so is Jack."

"Oh, my God! Oh, no! Oh, God no!" she cried, staring at me in disbelief. "Oh, God, it's true, isn't it? That's what's bothering her, that's what she couldn't tell me!" She jumped to her feet and stood shaking. I got up and took both her hands in mine. I said nothing and after a while the shaking stopped. She kept looking off from side to side, unseeing. "So, are you here to protect us or something?" she asked.

"I'm going to try to find out why they were killed and if you and your mother are in danger as your uncle seemed to think—which is the reason she has you both in hiding. Whether there is cause for fear, and how imminent any danger might be, I have no way of knowing, but your mom is taking it seriously and you need to also. She obviously thought that the less you knew the better. I disagree. If someone is out there looking for you, we all have to keep aware and cautious."

Natalie sat down. "You mean," she whispered, "someone might be looking for us here?"

"I don't know, Natalie, I honestly don't know, but I mean to find out and I need your help."

Once Jasmine was over the initial shock of her brother's death, which I broke to her as soon as we returned to the house. Natalie helped me console her mother and convinced her of the wisdom of my decision. "I mean, really mother, how long do you think you could keep me locked up?" Natalie teased her gently. And it was clear that Jasmine was relieved that she no longer had to bear the burden on her own.

Later that evening we sat down and Natalie started to talk. "Uncle Tony used to tell me about this bunch of Italian guys he knew. They used to all go to this club. It was like a bar, but only certain people went there. He used to say that some of them weren't very nice. Like, they did illegal gambling and sold stolen stuff. Like, I think, like, he wanted to shock me."

"Did you visit him in Houston?" I asked.

"Only a couple of times," Natalie replied. "You remember, Mom? He paid for me to take the bus down for Sandra's birthday. You remember her, don't you? She was really beautiful. I wanted to be an air hostess after I met her. He brought her up to Wimberley once and she invited me. She was his girlfriend for quite a while. I forget the other time."

"Do you think you might have ever met one of those friends of his?" I asked.

"Maybe at the party—I don't remember, but there were a lot of people there. It was in this big house that, like, had a pool and big game room. There was this guy who was, like, around seventeen. I think he was the son of one of Uncle Tony's friends. He was kind of flirting with me. He didn't know I was like fourteen or something then," she giggled.

"You never told me about that," said her mother.

"It wasn't anything, Mom," Natalie told her.

"Do you remember his name? Would you recognize him again?" I asked.

"I don't know if I would. I think his name was like, Dino, or something like that."

I turned to Jasmine. "You said that a friend from here gave you my number—who was that?

"Actually, she's a friend of our friend Tom who lives in Wimberley but has a house here in Port Aransas."

"So, she knows you are here?"

"Yes, but she doesn't know where. I found this place on my own after we got down here," Jasmine replied.

"Still, it might be good to think about moving to someplace where no-one knows you: Ingleside, or North Padre both have fairly transient populations—more anonymous," I told them.

We left it there and I drove back to Corpus.

Chapter 7

*Houston—where Grey begins to feel that
something could go good or horribly bad*

Tony Vigliano had lived in the Montrose, off Westheimer in a fairly modest apartment complex that was near his office on Kirby Drive. Most of his clients were the rich folks who lived a little further up the road in the River Oaks area. The place was closed and the neighbors on either side only knew that the owner had died. One of the girls in the bakery thought that it had been locked until his estate was settled, but no-one knew for sure.

Discreet enquiries by Kate to the local precinct officer in charge of the case revealed that, having been unable to contact the deceased's nearest and, as far as could be ascertained, only relative, namely Jasmine, they had shelved the case pending the unlikely possibility that someone might decide to open it again later.

Natalie, bless her little heart, had hung onto her phone after closing out her account. A search of calls made and calls received, amazingly, turned up Sandra's number. That girl threw nothing away. Her mother should be proud.

I had Natalie call Sandra on my phone and introduce me. After much evasion and half-truths, I was able to convince her to meet me the following Monday.

We met at the Houston terminal. She was still working for United. She looked like she had just come out of makeup, ready for her scene. How is it that air hostesses always look like air hostesses? We found a reasonably quiet place to sit, no small accomplishment. George Bush Intercontinental Airport, (it always seems like a mistake to me to name airports for presidents, particularly while they're still alive, but we're stuck with it now), like all international hubs, was a city in itself: anxious people running one way and then back; people trying to find a way to kill time between flights; constant noise, with annoying announcements often overlapping so that they're impossible to understand. Tony had had a bit of a gambling habit, had spent far too much time with "the guys" and apparently Sandra didn't like them, which was the reason she had stopped seeing him. I asked her if she remembered a kid named Dino that Natalie had met at a birthday party of hers.

"Boy! That was a few years ago," she exclaimed. "Yes, I remember he was very taken with her. I do see him around every so often. He's a sweet guy, actually. It's unfortunate that he was born into that life. I know he wishes he could get out, but you don't just quit those guys. You know what I mean?"

I nodded. "Do you know where I might find him? Have a photo by any chance?"

"Well, he does go to Tito's." She flipped open her phone and soon found pictures from the party. It had been memorable enough to hang on to some of them. "He hasn't changed that much," she said, holding the phone up for me to see. He was dark-haired, almost pretty, with a confident, teenage smirk on his face. "I guess there's no chance I can convince you to stay away from that place," she said resignedly. "Just be very careful, and I do mean very. And, whoever you are, give Natalie a hug for me when you see her." I promised I would.

It was inevitable the town just being laid out near the site of the battle of San Jacinto in 1836 should be named for General Sam Houston. His forces had just slaughtered the Mexican Army in the battle where the San Jacinto River and Buffalo Bayou come together. General Santa Anna's ruthless attack on the Alamo had whipped the Texans into a, "take no prisoners" fury, though Santa Anna survived to serve as Mexico's Emperor several more times. In 1866 he even turned to the United States thinking they might help him depose the Emperor Maximilian and get to rule Mexico once more. Lured to New York, he spent time imprisoned on Staten Island, not one to be idle, even in exile, Santa Anna introduced Chicle, the sap of the Sapodilla tree, hoping to make some money. An inventor, Thomas Adams, tried to make a substitute for rubber with it, after he gave up on that, he added flavoring and sweeteners and came up with chewing gum creating a company second only to Wrigley's.

The Republic of Texas was proclaimed, even though no nation recognized it and Mexico continued to try to get it back. When Sam Houston was elected President the town of Houston was named the Capital of Texas. That didn't last long and the capital was moved to the new town of Waterloo which was renamed Austin, for Stephen F. Austin, the "Father of Texas." Houston as a port flourished nevertheless, its importance never faltered though it wasn't until 1901, that it really took off. That was when Spindletop blew its 100-ft gush of oil into the Texas sky, bringing tens of thousands of fortune-seekers. The oil companies formed in Beaumont: Gulf, Humble, which became Exxon, and Texas, which became Texaco, moved their headquarters and shipping operations to Houston, and the place has been going ever since. The Buffalo Bayou, from Galveston Bay into the city, was dredged and widened into the Houston Ship Channel. If you care to venture through the wasteland of refineries and tank ponds down that way, you will find the battleground site where the San Jacinto monument and museum now stand.

Houston is huge, or as you are more likely to hear, "Youston is youge." I wouldn't choose to come here for my health, but it is home to the world's largest concentration of healthcare and research institutes, not to mention NASA'S mission control center, named for another Texas president, Lyndon Baines Johnson. Naturally, with its Texas-size concentration of wealth, it has great museums and theater districts and many terrific restaurants. Did I mention shopping? Well, let's just say I wouldn't let Kate loose in this town. Like all large cities, it's really an accumulation of villages, towns, neighborhoods and developments. The new, the old, the run-down, the upscale, ever-changing, morphing from the place where no one wants to live into the place where everyone wants to be seen. With the weakest zoning laws and preservation laws of any big city in the country, even buildings on the National Register of Historic Places can be erased if developers deem it necessary. Personally, if I have to go there, I stick pretty much to the Rice Village—it's quiet and pleasant. Westheimer is nearby, it has everything one could possibly want or need and it gets me well away from downtown before I hit the interstate.

I found Tito's a few blocks south of Westheimer in one of those neighborhoods you wouldn't go unless you really had to.

I checked out the immediate few blocks so that I would know my options if I had to make a quick exit, then walked into Tito's. The plain, nondescript exterior didn't prepare me for the interior, which strived for a certain elegance that it didn't quite pull off, but it was clean and didn't stink of beer and tobacco, a blessing in itself. As expected at that hour in the afternoon, the place was empty. I bought a coke which I rarely drink and a shot of rum, just to make it look like I was a drinker, which I am not, found a table in the corner near the entrance and tried to look like I was a salesman making out orders or a tout figuring who owed me and who I owed, while nursing the soda. After an hour, two men, who looked like extras from "Goodfellas," walked in and, barely greeting the barman, made their way through a door at the back of the room.

Fifteen minutes later another man walked in. Bingo! It was my lucky day. Dino, a little heavier all round, but definitely my man. As he went to sit at the bar, I gathered up my papers and walked out. From a coffee house across the road I watched and waited. Another hour went by before Dino left the bar and started down the street. I followed him from the other side. There were a few other pedestrians so I didn't stand out. When he turned at the first corner I hurried across and came up on him just as he was opening the door of a late model Lexus.

"Hello, Dino," I said.

He looked up in surprise and said, "Do I know you?"

"No," I said, "but if you would read this perhaps you will want to," I continued, handing him a piece of paper. The note said 'Hi Dino, this is

Natalie from Wimberley, "What's going on?"'
Apparently, the Marvin Gaye number had played a
lot at the party and Natalie thought it might be an
additional reminder.

"What the hell is this?" he scowled.

"For the sake of appearances, and I assume
you might be concerned about who might see you
speaking to a stranger, if you will wave in one
direction or other, as if you are giving me
directions, I will ball up this piece of paper, throw
it on the ground and walk away," I said. "If you
care about Natalie at all, she hopes you will phone
the number you probably saw there."

I could see that it had dawned on him who
Natalie was. I screwed up the paper, threw it
down and walked off in the direction he had
pointed. I didn't look back so there would be no
knowing if he would call until he did. At midnight
my phone rang.

"Just who are you, mister?" It was Dino's
voice.

"That's not important," I said. "I assume you
know what is planned for Natalie and her mother.
The fact that you called suggests you do, so let's
not bother taking the time to play. Write down
this other number I'm going to give you and, when
you learn anything, call it and simply say "They
have been found." That's all, and you will have
done possibly the best thing you ever did in your
life." I read out the number, there was a pause
then he hung up. I knew that the chances Dino

would or could break the code of *omerta*, the code of silence, pounded into Mafia families from the word go, was unlikely at best. However, he had called. That, in itself, was a sign that perhaps Sandra's assessment of Dino as being at odds with his Mafioso life and the possibility that his feelings for Natalie were sufficiently strong, gave me hope.

Chapter 8

Where a walk on the beach is not just a walk on the beach

Jasmine and Natalie had decided that they preferred Port Aransas to the alternatives. They had agreed that they could be just as safe or unsafe wherever they went and didn't want to keep running and hiding. It didn't take long to know who the locals were, Pt. A has a small population which is outnumbered by day tourists, fishing and sailing enthusiasts, vacationers and snow-birds. A good place to go unnoticed most of the time.

After a chance conversation on the beach with a student at the Marine Science Institute, which is part of the University of Texas at Austin, Natalie decided to check out its Animal Rehabilitation Keep.

The ARK, as it is known, is located on the grounds of the Institute but, is largely funded by people concerned about the fate of animals impacted by man's activities on and near the waters of the Gulf of Mexico, its estuaries, bays and the rivers that feed into the gulf. Natalie learned there was a constant need for help with the daily feeding and care of the ARK's sea turtles, coastal birds and just about any other wild critter that might turn up injured or lost: preparing food, feeding animals, cleaning cages and working on the general upkeep of the facilities, some of which was done by the Institute maintenance crew, but the bulk of which required the constant assistance of dedicated volunteers.

After an initial squeamishness over cleaning up bird feces (it amazed her how much one bird could produce in a day), she found she really enjoyed the work and developed a strong attachment to the turtles. Some animals were resident due to injuries that precluded their ever being released to the wild. This included a great blue heron which had amazingly recovered from a broken leg but, once released, chose to hang around, always showing up at feeding time. Those that came and went, successfully rehabilitated, felt like a personal triumph, even while knowing that her part in their recovery was minimal.

For her part, Jasmine hooked up with members of the non-profit organization, "Friends of the ARK", the group dedicated to increasing public awareness and raising money for the ARK's work. The public release of turtles back into the gulf always drew a crowd and volunteers were also needed there to sell t-shirts, answer questions and generally help out. She often didn't have the answers, (though she had learned a little, thanks to Natalie's enthusiastic embrace of the ARK's mission), the aim was to recruit more volunteers. Jasmine gladly assisted in this.

Though wary of contact with too many people, they both had learned to make an almost unconscious assessment of their surroundings and of those around them. At the same time, these activities managed to take their minds off of the '800lb. gorilla' lurking out there. It was also not possible for them to contact any friends. Most upsetting for Jasmine was the thought of all her things back in Wimberley. The things she had accumulated over the years, her plants and the house itself. Their home. They had the bare necessities, clothes from the used clothing store in town, little else. The house she had rented was furnished with well-worn furniture and beds that weren't the most comfortable, a sparsely equipped kitchen with pots and pans that had probably been thrown out from the owners' kitchen. Betsy had volunteered to check on the house in Wimberley while Jasmine was in Sicily, whether she had continued to do so after hearing nothing from Jasmine for so long was impossible to know.

I checked on them every morning and evening. Jasmine would wander along the shoreline, intent on shells, she had started making jewelry using the shells collected on the beach along with various other odds and ends that caught her attention on these morning walks. I would stroll along in the opposite direction until we were close enough to hear each other and, as she went by, I would stop, as if arrested by the behavior of the gulls, terns or any of the other shorebirds nearby. This afforded me the opportunity to see if anyone appeared to be particularly interested in this lady on the beach. They were both to call me if either of them happened to see anything suspicious. Now thoroughly adept at being fully aware of where they were, of who was around and what escape routes were available should it become necessary. The summer was coming to an end and it was beginning to seem that it had all been just a bad dream. Perhaps there was a time limit to how long a group, even one as persistent as the Mafia, would continue such a seemingly unimportant pursuit.

***

Then Kate got the call, "They found them." Dino had shown himself to be a good guy and very likely a courageous one also. There was no more than that so, I went into 24-hour surveillance mode. Whether they had narrowed it down to just Pt. A, where they actually lived or any details, was impossible to know. At least I wasn't doing that drive twice a day. Now, Kate drove over after work so that we could spend the night together even if I didn't always sleep. We continued the beach routine. The end of summer meant there were less people around. Picking a killer out of men who happened to be down there, was just as big a task as guessing whether it would be the same man as the man from Sicily, who I felt I had a pretty good idea I could pick out, based on Jasmine's description. It could just as easily be a non-Italian looking substitute. Who knew if it was even a man I was looking for. My bird-watching allowed me to swivel in both directions following a bird's flight and surveying the beach in both directions from dunes to the water. Tense days went by.

We had switched to three times a day for these encounters, so very early one morning found us again converging on the beach. Jasmine was walking from the jetty end of the beach. The jetty defined the end of Mustang Island where the ship channel took boats into Corpus Christi Bay, to the docks and oil refineries. I, of course, was headed toward her. It looked as though we would meet more or less in front of the I.B. Magee Park headquarters. There was still a fairly thick morning haze, the kind that occurs at the change of the seasons. The top viewing deck of the Park building was where a friend of mine does his yoga stretches and sun salutations during his morning walk. It would also afford someone with a high-powered rifle command of that stretch of the beach and its certainly not difficult to come by a weapon. but I clung to the belief that that didn't fit the *modus operandi* of the Mafia. They seemed to revel in the up-close, visceral experience of dealing death. The fact is, of course, death by any and all means is how they proceed, but I didn't want to think along those lines.

A figure wearing a light blue track suit stepped out of the shadow on the top deck and was either staring out to sea or looking intently at Jasmine. I picked up my pace and, as I approached her, said, "Don't stop, keep going to the pier," and moved on by. A little further along, I turned away from the water's edge, made my way up the beach and started back. I couldn't see if anyone was upstairs and was momentarily at a loss as to what to do. Then I saw a man emerge from one of the port-a-potties strung along that part of the beach by the dunes where vehicles drive. He was carrying a bundle and wore one of those Speedo swim suits that only Europeans wear to the beach, as if they were about to compete in the Olympics. The overhanging belly and display of too much pubic hair tends to spoil the illusion. I stayed back and followed him as he went towards the pier. I couldn't see Jasmine and hoped that she had found a safe place to hide. At the foot of the ramp to the pier the man set his bundle down and started up the ramp. It was then that I saw Jasmine walking down the pier. She must have thought I had said, 'go onto the pier.' Usually, at that time of the morning, there would be at least a couple of intrepid fishermen out at the end of the pier, but this morning it was empty. As I started down the pier the man glanced back, evidently calculating that he had enough of a start to do what he was there for and then deal with me—he started to jog.

I started to run, faster than I had in, probably 30 years. Mustang Island is the longest barrier island in the world, the Horace Caldwell pier is only 400 yards long but it seemed like the longest pier in the world at that point. Whether I could overcome his head start was the gut-wrenching question. The roar of the surf, the screech of the gulls all disappeared; even the thud of my feet on the decking was imperceptible. My entire being was concentrated on one thing only, reaching that guy before he got to Jasmine. I was desperate, my client, who, to tell the truth, had, along with Natalie, become not only someone I cared for but a life that I felt duty bound to save. Yet here I was about to witness her death. Jasmine reached the end of the pier, there was nowhere to go. She turned to face her pursuer. I was not going to make it. As if in a nightmare I saw the glint of the sun off the knife in his right hand as the assassin lunged at her, his hand swung towards her throat. With perfect timing, as if she had practiced a hundred times, in a split second, Jasmine squatted to the floor bringing her arms up to protect her face. The man's advance carried him over her head into the surround rail. Jasmine kicked out at his feet and for a moment he teetered, almost see-sawing on the rail, just as I was there to grab the back of his trunks and heave up with all my strength. As he doubled over the guard rail, his face hit the concrete base of the rail with a sickening crunch and he cart-wheeled down into the sea. Suddenly, all the sounds returned; the waves striking the pilings supporting the pier, the gulls protesting this disturbance of their space. I pulled Jasmine to her feet, the shock showing in her eyes probably not much greater than mine and without a look back hustled her down the pier. We were both trembling; me from exertion and Jasmine from fear. There was a young couple now down by the entrance, too intent on each other to spare us a glance. "Well fuck you, shithead," I heard her say as we passed them. I guess people will never learn to get along. I picked up the clothing the man had left, took the wallet and put the rest into the White Trash Co. dumpster by the parking lot.

***

Just to satisfy my own curiosity about the motivations of the relentless pursuit of Jasmine, I contacted Sandra again and together with what she conjectured, information gleaned from some of my own and Kate's sources in Houston, pieced together what seemed to be the most plausible explanation.

It runs like this: One of Tony's more dubious associates asked him to recommend a realtor who would act on behalf of some Italian 'businessmen' wanting to invest in construction in Houston. The realtor would find and buy the property on their behalf and, as their representative, handle all contracts and negotiations with architects, construction companies, banks and permitting authorities. Tony's friend Jack was happy to take on the task.

Happy, that is, until it dawned on them both that the financing of the project was coming from Italian government funds intended for the construction of subsidized housing for the poor in Naples, siphoned off by mafiosi council members and crooked contractors. That's when Jack Fellini retired to the Hill Country. Fellini's departure caused the whole project to collapse so there were some very unhappy and poorer gentlemen who were not gentlemen. They were not about to let an affront of this kind go by without notice. The seeds of what followed were sown at that time.

Tony had claimed total ignorance of the entire proceedings, but both must have known, deep down, that there would be some kind of consequences for their involvement. It was clear that it was on Jack Fellini's mind when he reluctantly agreed to go to Sicily. Whether they both knew they were living on borrowed time is hard to say. Unless one had a fairly thorough knowledge of the Mafia and their methods, one might be inclined to think that minor brushes with their activities would be overlooked. My studies suggested otherwise.

The writer Leonardo Sciascia managed to live all his life in Racalmuto in Sicily *and* write about the Mafia. Although he confessed that any cutting, or editing of his work wasn't done for artistic or literary reasons but, rather so as to, "Fend off the possible intolerance of those who might consider themselves more or less directly attacked by my representation." In other words, be careful what you say. It could get you into a lot of trouble. The possibility that one might know something about a particular crime could be enough to put one in danger of losing one's life. This, it would seem, was the sole reason for Jack's and Tony's death and the pursuit of Jasmine.

Chapter 9

Everything is wrapped up. Maybe

"I see another John Doe showed up on the beach in Port A," Kate said, when she called that evening. "Know anything about it?" I had, up to that moment, managed to keep my mind focused on other things. There was always the chance that a Hammerhead, Bull, Tiger or one of the other variety of sharks that have been caught off the pier, might have disposed of the body. That would be a tidy way to wrap things up but, instead, there would be enquiries, investigations, expenditure of tax-payer's money; all to discover the identity of a low-life, low tier, member of a criminal organization who had been prevented from committing the crime of murder.

During my late-night surveillances, I had been reading a book about cosmology, the universe and all the weird science that has come to light in pursuit of knowledge. A great deal of the book was incomprehensible to me. Quantum Physics, however, made perfect sense. Quantum

Physics revealed that the observer plays a role in the observed.

The way I understand it: Depending on how you examine them, subatomic particles will sometimes resemble particles, sometimes waves. While the two images are mathematically equivalent they are not really one thing or the other because the act of observation influences the qualities that they present to us. As the author Tim Ferris puts it, in *Coming of Age in the Milky Way*, what previously has been a philosophical consideration, quantum physics obliges us to take seriously: That we do not see things in themselves, but only aspects of things.

"Well, darling," I said, "to the best of my knowledge only three people saw the incident. One is dead and you'd have to ask the other participant their view of events. From my present personal perspective, I'd have to say that the man committed suicide: plain and simple. He should never have been out there at that time and place. As they say: 'Things could look different in the morning." I concluded.

"And the morning after that too, I suppose?" said Kate.

Chapter 10

Matt Grey raises philosophical questions about the law

'Be not deceived.' Most people would have said 'Don't kid yourself.' Men, more often than not, would add, 'buddy.' Buddy, in this case, would be intended to add an additional dismissive or patronizing note to the statement. The 'buddy', not as 'friend,' but carrying all the prejudice of class: You're no better than me. Don't give yourself airs. 'Be not deceived' was more like a Confucian maxim: a rule to live by, a timely warning given with concern and sympathy, lacking any sense that the speaker was wiser or superior in any way. While there might be a certain archaic sound to it, 'Be not deceived' carried more weight; it stuck with you. Made you think. Had I deceived myself? Was I about to deceive myself? Was it fair warning or merely, not merely, solely, a suggestion that in the course of whatever I undertook to do about the situation, I be clearheaded, aware? Aware that decisions we make are based on subjective, narrow and often misleading information, interpretations of facts, part fact, and even fiction. Facts can be twisted into fiction or fiction can become fact if it suits our interpretation. What we want or do not want to be the truth. Heady stuff; especially when you're in my business. We like it cut and dried: right and wrong, guilty or not guilty. The facts are... they prove this.

When it comes to crime, much of the time it's pretty simple stuff. The guy is caught red-handed with the stolen goods. The guy is driving a stolen car. The guy is selling drugs. There are witnesses. There are so many clues a 10-year-old could figure it out. Some cases are trickier. It takes some investigation. Questions have to be asked, leads followed. The everyday criminal is pretty dumb though. They're not thinking ahead. Not thinking things through. No planning, usually. Of course, a lot of crimes go unsolved. There's not enough police in the world to handle all the crimes committed. The professional criminal knows this. If more people knew it, there might be even more crime. As it is, it seems half the population is stealing from the other half.

Cops & Robbers is one thing, though. Deviants, the criminally insane, that's something else. And laws discriminate against certain members of society. I wasn't supposed to think that way when I was a cop; sworn to uphold the law. It's true though: lawmakers decide what constitutes a crime. Crime & Punishment—that wasn't my department; cops enforce the laws— Plain and Simple. The prosecutors, the lawyers and the judicial system decide the punishment. It's all subject to interpretation though. Again, I wasn't supposed to go there. But you don't have to be on the job long before it is pretty clear that some people get away with murder, figuratively and literally. Money talks, power walks—makes you a little cynical at times. I'd thought about quitting many times. But it's a job and most of the time it's straight forward and simple. Even when you think some of the laws are stupid. We catch you breaking the law, you're busted. It's just a job. Then I was invalided out of the force (never try to talk a meth-head with a gun into being reasonable). That's when I went into business for myself: private detection.

Anyway, that was the phrase that popped into my head that night, after getting Jasmine settled. The fact is, she had taken the whole thing better than me. Where she felt triumphant, having rid herself of her worst nightmare, I was shaken by the fact that I had almost lost my client in the worst possible way. Not to mention that I was faced with what you might call a moral dilemma. If I were to inform the authorities, as was my civic duty, a round of legal proceedings would begin with no-knowing how they would end or when and at what cost. My involvement in the whole episode had put me in the position whereby, I could subject myself, Jasmine and Natalie, and even Kate, to years of court appearances, enormous lawyer's fees and the draining stress of never being allowed to leave it behind.

Furthermore, if the case were to attract news-coverage, it could reach the ears of those who had set the whole thing in motion. The endless pursuit of the vendetta, that consumed generations of Sicilians, loomed high and would haunt us all for the rest of our lives, if what we had learned in the process of the case held true, no matter how much we might wish it to be otherwise. Was I to go to the authorities, tell them all I knew and throw Jasmine, Natalie, myself and Kate into months, if not years, of legal hassles and expense. All for some low-life, low ranking Mafia murderer who very likely deserved to die several times over for crimes committed? Not only that but, should an inquiry get sufficient publicity, somewhere, in the dark corners of the Mafia world, revenge might be deemed necessary. The hunt for Jasmine taken up again, while my involvement could be considered an offense that might necessitate my elimination. Better John Doe remain John Doe. No one was likely to turn up to claim the body, that's for sure.

I've definitely made harder decisions.

***

While there was no way of knowing how long Jack's gift would continue to provide for Jasmine, she took it as a sign that she should leave while she could. Go as far away as possible. To one of the exotic places she had dreamed of living. Where, in time, the events of the past few months would seem to have happened in another lifetime. Jasmine was set on being a full-time jewelry maker. The skills she had developed while in Port Aransas had convinced her that she could earn a living that way and besides, she had tapped into a creative side of herself she never knew was there. Natalie was determined to dedicate her life to saving turtles and protecting the ocean. With the help of our lawyer friend Jim Houston, I would discretely devise a way to enable Betsy to sell the Wimberley house and deposit the money into an account that Jasmine would have access to. While letting Betsy know her dearest friend, while unable to communicate, had not abandoned her.

We decided it were best if we didn't keep in touch, although she could always find me. Kate and I drove them to the airport when they left. It was good to see them both happy and positive. The haunted look was no longer apparent. Jasmine had survived, her 'give peace a chance' self still intact, and back in place. They were a resilient pair. I had no doubt that they would find a home, wherever they went.

After much discussion and research, Jasmine and Natalie had decided to move to . . . Well, I better not say. Just in case.

###

BONUS!

The following short story entitled "R.I.P." is provided as a bonus in this edition of "BE NOT DECEIVED"

Cover design by Michael Earney, Jason Muñoz, and Lynn Amos

Painting ("Rogelio" from the Roadside Memorial Series) by Michael Earney

R.I.P.

The man thought he would take a walk. He'd been sitting most of the day. He had read the paper, not much to that; done the crossword, it was a weekday so there wasn't much to that either. He solved the word jumble by guessing the answer before unjumbling all the encrypted letters. He had found eighty-six words in the word for the day—"redaction" —in under an hour and had given up on the Sudoku fairly quickly. He wasn't a numbers man. He hadn't taken his usual morning walk. Having risen slightly later than usual, the decision to have breakfast first, a rare thing, and a certain reluctance to go out, had meant that by the time he decided to go the sun was already pouring out its summer heat, which in Texas always seems to be more enervating than anywhere else, with, perhaps the exception of Bangkok, Thailand. He'd decided to wait until evening when it wouldn't necessarily be cooler, but the heat would, at least, be decreasing rather than increasing. A daily walk had become important to him, and just as his other habits and daily rituals, had become hardened routines.

His daily walk was an essential part of his life. He liked to think that he was not so rigid that some variation in routine was not only acceptable, but laudable; however, he rarely missed this part of his practice. The fact that he had done so on this day was particularly noteworthy. Often, especially in winter, the time of year he abhorred, due to his Raynaud's syndrome—a condition which causes some areas of the body such as fingers and toes to feel numb and cold in response to cold temperatures, where the small arteries that supply blood to the skin narrow and limit blood supply to the affected areas. He considered it an affliction, especially given the fact that those fortunate unafflicted, or those that were unaware of the condition, tended to view his reluctance to expose himself to the cold as a lack of backbone. Their inability to comprehend the pain suffered by those with the condition led them to scorn. Conversely, he had little sympathy for those that could not live through the Texas summer without air-conditioning, something he detested.

He felt, having read it somewhere, that as long as he walked most days of the week he was getting sufficient exercise, but just as some people think that taking more than the prescribed amount of a supplement, vitamin or drug will be better for them, he believed that the more he exercised the healthier he would be. Like many people as they age, he had become more concerned about his health and physical condition and consequently dedicated more time and thought to the process of trying to preserve them. One look in the mirror, and taking note of how he felt in the morning when he rose, was enough to tell him that no matter what he did there was no reversing the condition of ageing. It often seemed to him that all the effort, time and money spent on the subject had little if any effect. Still, once set on the path, the thought that things would be infinitely worse should he stop, and one look around at how decrepit and unhealthy the majority of people were, spurred him on in his regime.

His walk, though not invariable, took one of three alternative routes, all of which steered clear of heavily trafficked streets. Breathing extra large amounts of carbon dioxide and all the other output of the internal combustion engine struck him as counter-productive. The quieter neighborhoods offered solitude and tranquility. Barking dogs were to be expected, but they rarely wandered the streets and, while annoying, presented little danger. Leash laws ensured that dogs being walked by their owners were kept under a degree of control. Never having been a dog-lover he couldn't bring himself to use these animals as an excuse for interaction with their owners, even if at times he might welcome the opportunity. Faking an interest in their dog didn't seem like a good way to meet someone and, generally speaking, he found dog-lovers to be of a sensibility at odds with his own. Accosting other dog-less walkers, beyond a "good morning" or "hello" was socially more difficult, if not frowned upon, and not being an outgoing person, was a rare occurrence. When these interactions did occur, chances were the accoster was either looking for a handout—less likely in the neighborhoods he frequented—lost, or some older person, garrulous to the point of mental instability, to be shunned or disengaged from as quickly as possible.

On this particular evening, aside from the occasional vehicle, he had the streets to himself. He wondered when these well-kempt front yards were worked on. He never saw anyone mowing, weeding or trimming, planting or watering. Once inside their homes, it seemed the owners only exited to get into their vehicles, to pick up the daily paper resting on their driveways, or to retrieve mail from the box by the street. Could there be a system of interconnected backyards where neighbors socialized, exchanged information and solidified their attitudes toward politics, religion, ethics and prejudices? Instinctively, he knew that nine out of ten of these households held opinions on all these subjects diametrically opposed to his own. How such uniformity of attitude came about was a mystery to him. His upbringing had been relatively normal, but he had developed an early alienation from his family and from society in general. Not that this was so unusual. It was, in fact, a common phase to go through: teenage angst. Except, instead of growing out of it, getting a nine-to-five job, getting married and settling down to a life much like that of his parents, he gravitated to the arts, philosophy, anti-establishment activists and outsiders. While these interests aligned him with a large segment of the population involved in such activities, his lack of formal education, training, shyness, diffidence and little self-regard, kept him from ever fully engaging those with whom he had the most in common. He was a solitary man, at odds with practically all established forms of social intercourse.

He turned left on leaving the house and at the end of the street, right, taking him up the hill that led to the cemetery. As the elevation increased, views of the town and surrounding countryside could be glimpsed between the houses and trees. The mournful sound of a freight train's horn carried across the valley as it approached road crossings, adding to the melancholic stillness of the neighborhood. He only now noticed that the morning's clear blue sky had given way to increasing cloud, and that the sun, hidden by some dark and rain-heavy clouds, might not appear again until dusk. He guessed that the chance of rain was unlikely and pressed on up the steepening hill the road followed. The way into the cemetery from this street was through a narrow space in the fence, deliberately left in the far southwest corner. It was a narrow space, barely wide enough for a person to pass through. It opened into trees alongside the road. Although there was a well-worn path leading there and was barely seven feet from the road, most passersby would not notice it. He supposed that it was primarily intended for the White-tailed Deer that frequented the grounds.

Once inside the fence he was careful not to step inside the concrete dividers delineating the burial plots. These low, perhaps six-inch-high by four-inch-wide walls fenced the plot with a grassy space of about two feet separating each plot from another. The plots came in four sizes, the smallest accommodating two headstones. These headstones were mostly uniform in size and shape, a grey granite pillow, smoothed and sometimes polished on one side where the name and date of the deceased's birth and death were carved. These, judging by their uniformity, could be part of the package offered by the cemetery. Naturally, many of the large plots displayed the wealth or ostentation of the bereaved with marble monuments, obelisks, weeping angels, crypts, etc. The cemetery covered forty-five acres at the top of a hill. The long driveway, running down to the entrance off the highway, was intersected with drives to access all parts of the grounds; these had names like, 'Remembrance Drive' and 'Memory Lane', rather like a subdivision, so that visitors would know where to find their departed loved ones. A deer lifted her head at his approach while her two fawns, still in their spotted coats, browsed unaware. Gauging that the man was far enough away to offer no threat, the doe, after stamping her foot once, went back to her business. In the parched, stony, juniper-covered hill country, the cemetery was an oasis for wildlife, regularly watered expanses of green, exotic trees and the occasional bouquet of real flowers offered abundance in this hard-scrabble land. Having walked briskly down several lanes, scaring up other deer that cantered away, the man began to dawdle, looking at the grave markers, their grey uniformity relieved only by the different names, decorative addition if there were any, and the occasional quotation, usually biblical or sentimental, mostly banal, of the 'Gone but not forgotten' variety.

The Friends of the Cemetery, a non-profit organization for the beautification and enhancement of the cemetery, encouraged bequests, endowments and donations which enabled the planting of trees and the removal of ball moss from the old and venerable Live Oak trees, ensuring that the entire property had the cared for look of a park. Even the oldest graves, though presumably no longer visited, did not have the neglected, long-forgotten look that overtakes so many cemeteries. The first recorded burial was in 1876. However, slaves of the earliest settlers had been buried there prior to that date. An earlier city cemetery, closer to town, had proved too small, hence the move to its present location which, thanks to the city's growth, was now hemmed in by houses. Many of the older cemetery's residents had been part of the move, consequently, there were headstones bearing dates from long before the first burial in the new cemetery—Texas pioneers, veterans of the war of 1812 and of the Texas Revolution, 1835-1836. The man found himself in front of just such a one: Cpt. John T. Holland, Confederate States Army, Feb. 1836 - Dec. 1900, flanked by another bearing the dates 1823-1857.

Coming to the Serenity Garden, he stopped to sit down on one of the stone benches and looked across the highway that bounded the cemetery on one side, to the university. "Dare," he thought, suddenly. That would make it 87. How had he missed that one? Too late now of course, but it bothered him. "Dare"—he hadn't dared much in his life. Perhaps that was why it hadn't come to him before. Always cautious, seeking the safer way, seldom spontaneous or reckless, his life had dribbled away to this, walking alone in a cemetery. Many of his friends were dead or disappeared from his life. They didn't contact him, he didn't contact them. On the other hill, across the highway, 3400 students vied for bachelor's, master's and doctoral degrees, full of ambition, hope and endeavor. Youngsters from around the world came to this seat of learning. It had opened in 1903 as the Southwest Texas State Normal School, just blocks from downtown, going through four name changes as it spread up the hill, and now boasting 218 buildings with others under construction. It was an attractive campus. The second largest natural spring in Texas rose on its grounds and the San Marcos River proceeded from it, winding its way through six acres of campus grounds, bordered by stately Cypress and Pecan trees. Its grassy banks were a favorite hangout for students: swimming, snorkeling and sunbathing. Young bodies of every shape and size were on display. Basketball and volleyball courts, picnic and barbeque areas were alive with energy. There was more to campus life than study. It was the only university in Texas that could boast of having graduated a U.S. president, Lyndon Baines Johnson.

The man was tired, but noted that the sun was close to setting; clouds had gathered, and he shivered though it was far from cold. Drawing himself to his feet, he set out for a path that would lead back to the corner of the cemetery where he could exit to the road below. Once again he glanced at the gray, old stones bearing names no longer common: Ezell, Sevey, Wash, Coovert, Tittle, and Puls, with dates from the 18th and 19th century, just as were many of the first names: Beatrice, Zachariah, Malachi and Erasmus, seldom now heard. Whether all these long dead had opted to pay the 'perpetual care' fee or if zealous grounds people took it upon themselves to keep all neat and tidy, it was clear this cemetery had no place for discarded wreaths, old flowers or any kind of trash or weeds. It was a place very much for the dead and not the living. Why the dead should take up so much space was a mystery to the man. Acres and acres of land set aside for the purpose of burying bodies.

How had this fixation on somehow preserving the remains of the dead lodged itself so firmly in the mind of man? Not the Hindu, of course, they simply burned copious amounts of wood then sent their ashes downstream. Not the North American Plains Indian or the Tibetans. Still there was much ritual and memorializing even with them. And monuments! The Valley of Tombs, the Tal Mahal, the Albert Memorial. The Chinese Emperor Qin Shi Huang was buried in a necropolis complex replicating his imperial palace, with workers, weapons, armor, tools, pottery— everything he had in life. Guarded, so he thought, for eternity by life-size terracotta figures of 8000 soldiers, 130 chariots pulled by 520 horses and 50 cavalry horses. All facing east where his conquered states lay. The site still has much to be uncovered. The temple of the inscriptions at Palenque, Mexico sits atop the largest eight-step pyramid in Meso-America. A rubble-filled passage was found in its floor. When cleared, it was found to lead down below ground level to a wall, behind which sacrificed attendants protected the entrance to a tomb containing a massive sarcophagus where lay the richly adorned body of Pacal, God-King of the Maya. The effort and energy given to make it appear that for some special people death has been defeated at the same time as Man slaughters his own kind by the millions and tramples their remains into the mud without a second thought, is extraordinary. What a strange creature, Man.

Now it was almost dark. Which way to the gap in the fence? He was momentarily disoriented before cutting across a plot—excuse me—to the track. He hurried along seeking familiar names that would satisfy him that he was headed in the right direction. Ahead rose the white marble 'Cleopatra's needle' marking the Whipple family plot. So many generations and yet rarely did he see new gravesites. Were they running out of space? Had this cemetery fallen out of favor? Were there more fashionable places to be buried these days? At the very time these thoughts crossed his mind, the telltale mound of fresh earth with a single, simple wreath and a temporary marker appeared ahead. Reaching it, the man paused to read the dedication:

Yesterday's date. Here lies William P. Drake. William P. Drake! Buried! Here!

William Drake fell to his knees, covered his face and wept.

R.I.P.

ABOUT THE AUTHOR

Michael Earney is a renowned fine arts painter and has been a commercial artist, tee-shirt designer, maker of one-of-a-kind decorative folding-screens and headboards, ceramic sculptor, a potter, and an award-winning documentary filmmaker.

He co-authored *Land and Cattle*; his paintings of Mexican masks are collected and published as *Magic Faces, Caras Magicas*, and he wrote the text which is in English and Spanish. His work is included in *Las Aves de los altos de Chiapas* and *La Pitahaya en las Artes Plasticas*, and has contributed both artwork and writing to a variety of publications.

CONNECT WITH THE AUTHOR

www.MichaelEarney.com

www.EarneyWorks.com

www.facebook.com/themichaelearney

www.smashwords.com/profile/view/meartist37

www.amazon.com/author/themichael37

www.fineartamerica.com/profiles/michael-earney.html

OTHER TITLES BY MICHAEL EARNEY

Michael has written and illustrated:

The A to Z Book of Birds
for Young Bird Lovers

While looking at my grand-daughter's books with her it occurred to me that here, at three years old, she can identify images which bear little resemblance to the actual creatures portrayed: whale, giraffe, ostrich, etc. At the zoo she recognizes the elephant, tiger, giraffe, etc. Why, I wondered, do children's books have such simplified renderings of animals? She may not be able to read the names, but she knows a giraffe is a giraffe. Her father is an avid birder and can barely wait to take her birding, so why not an alphabet book with realistic pictures of birds?

Thus, "The A to Z Book of Birds: An ABC for Young Bird Lovers" - she will know her birds before she knows her alphabet. I'm sure my grand-daughter is not the only three-year-old genius out there. This book is designed to be useful from age three to well beyond learning the alphabet, when the text, informative and entertaining, will continue to teach and the paintings be a guide to identification in the field.

The A to Z Book of Weeds and Other Useful Plants

Children have a natural curiosity about the world around them. When it comes to the world of nature, adults often can't help other than to say, 'Don't touch that!' 'Don't play with that!' or 'Don't eat that!' Of course, children will do all these things anyway. Therefore, simply, intriguingly, informatively, and I hope humorously, this book tries to introduce young and old alike to the plants around us that are considered to be a nuisance, worthless or potentially harmful: the weeds.

As we find, those plants that we don't want, and annually spend millions of dollars trying to eradicate, have served mankind for thousands of years and though we may not realize it, continue to provide food, medicine, shelter, clothing and pleasure to millions of people worldwide. If, seeing a bush or tree laden with fruit, you ever wondered, 'Can you eat those?' or have seen a beautiful tiny wildflower and wished you knew its name, this book will start you on a journey of discovery not to be missed, starting right outside your door.

The A to Z of Wildflowers

How many names of wildflowers do you know? Considering that there are 5000 flowering plants in Texas at least a thousand of which can be called 'wild flowers' it's safe to say, not many.

The beginners guide will, I hope, help to put names to some of the more common ones, give impetus to search for the uncommon ones and provide information about some of the interesting plants around us. You will find names, locations and many little known facts that will entertain and enlighten. The illustrations by author Michael P. Earney represent many years of enjoying the Texas outdoors.

Magic Faces – Caras Magicas:
Mexican Mask Paintings

The ancient intent and purpose of the animistic masks of the indigenous people of Mexico can yet be found in those used in dances and fiestas today. Set in the context of these paintings, the masks reveal themselves to be an essential part of the history and the culture of Mexico.

The A to Z Book of Did You Know:
Guaranteed Something You Didn't Know

This addition to the A to Z series delves into the realms of general and esoteric knowledge, things we should know, things we thought we knew and things you never before thought about.

It's a fun, eclectic collection that is guaranteed to provide many 'Gee whiz!' moments and interesting information with which you can stun friends and family alike.

Fittingly, the illustrations also come from a wide range of sources and will surprise and delight you. There is no doubt that owning this book will add to your knowledge, improve your diet and increase brain cells. Or your money back!

The A to Z Book of Cats,
Wild and Domestic

Want the purrr-fect gift for the cat lover in your life? Cat got your tongue? Never mind, the A to Z book of Cats will say it all for you. It's the cat's meow. Not only have cats found a place in our hearts and homes, but they are also part of our history, culture, and arts. This book with illustrations by the author, while it's not cat-a-clysmic, will appeal to all ailurophiles, (that's cat lovers). Failure to purchase this book would not be a cat-a-strophe and I certainly won't go cat-a-tonic but, if you do, I predict you will find yourself sitting in the catbird's seat wearing the cat's pajamas!

The A to Z Book of Mushrooms

Mushrooms, fungi, molds, mycorrhizal spores. These all affect you every day of your life. They have helped keep the world operating for millions of years. For thousands of years they have provided humans with the means to exist. The 5300yr. old "Iceman" found in the Alps in 1991 had two different mushrooms in his pouch that were important to his survival in the world. While you may not need them for your survival (if you did you might turn to that mold, penicillin), multiple ongoing studies into the medicinal properties of various mushrooms may soon add to the already proven ways mushrooms can save lives. You can certainly benefit from knowing your mushrooms. *The A to Z book of Mushrooms* will help you find and identify wild mushrooms. The illustrations and the text are designed to introduce beginners to the wonderful, colorful, nutritious and magical world of mushrooms.

HIS FICTIONAL WORKS INCLUDE:

Corpus

Corpus means there should be a body, and there is! Detective Matt Grey has to do some driving around South Texas, including Corpus Christi, Kingsville, Alice, and Port Aransas on Mustang Island, to find the connections surrounding a murder--or is it suicide? Malfeasance and family feuding will keep you page-turning.

Agla and Kevin

What if a band of Indians, not contacted since their ancestors retreated from the Spanish conquistadors, remained living in the Texas Hill Country? Young Kevin Jones, lost and injured, chances upon these people and begins a life unimaginably different from the one he has known. He learns the ways of living in harmony with nature and is opened to the strange and inexplicable world of shamanism.

More stories are being readied for publication.

www.ingramcontent.com/pod-product-compliance
Lightning Source LLC
Chambersburg PA
CBHW060754180626
46818CB00002B/566